SALUKI

HOUND OF THE BEDOUIN

STACEY INTERNATIONAL

Saluki, Hound of the Bedouin
published by
Stacey International
128 Kensington Church Street
London W8 4BH
Tel: 020 7221 7166 Fax: 020 7792 9288
E-mail: enquiries@stacey-international.co.uk
Website: www.stacey-international.co.uk

ISBN: 1-905299-00-1
CIP Data: A catalogue record for this book is available from the British Library

© Julia Johnson 2005
1 3 5 7 9 0 8 6 4 2

Design: Kitty Carruthers
Printing & Binding: SNP Leefung, China

Dedicated to Ben, Alice and William

SALUKI
HOUND OF THE BEDOUIN

Story by Julia Johnson

Illustrations by Susan Keeble

Acknowledgements

My grateful thanks to Hamad Ghanem Shaheen Al Ghanem for sharing his family history with me and for introducing me to the Arabian Saluki.

Hamad's family have been breeding Arabian Salukis since 1926. In 1980, he started the stud book of the Saluki of Arabia in Bahrain to register hounds and owners, and to trace the lineage and origins of the hound in the Gulf States. He is a well-known and respected judge of the Arabian Saluki in competitions.

He is the Founder and Director of the Arabian Saluki Centre 2002, Abu Dhabi, United Arab Emirates; Breeder and Registrar General of Saluki of Arabia; and Board Director of the Society for the Perpetuation of Desert Bred Salukis, Arizona, USA.

Hamad is aiming to gain recognition of the Arabian Saluki by establishing clubs to draw attention to the Arabian tradition of hunting with Salukis and falcons.

We are also indebted to David and Helen Graham of Daxlor kennels for their assistance, and for allowing us to photograph their Salukis.

Foreword

Readers of any age will enjoy this delightful story of Hamad and his Saluki, Sougha. Between them, Julia Johnson with her pen and Susan Keeble with her brush, have managed to capture so well the intimate relationship between the Bedouin of the desert and their hounds that has endured through centuries to the present day. Indeed, it is precisely this relationship that has endowed the desert-bred Saluki with the characterisitcs that make it so different from mere dogs.

As this story shows, the Saluki is essentially a working breed, probably the oldest in the world, with an ancestry stretching back into Mesopotamian history. Its primary task of hunting for the pot in the harsh environment of the desert calls for a disciplined hound of great speed and stamina. The Bedouin have developed a bond with their Salukis based on their mutual dependence for survival, such that the hounds seem to know what is required of them with hardly a word of command or even a gesture. Some find them aloof and undemonstrative, but in a Muslim society where ritual purification is necessary before praying if one has come into contact with an unclean animal (even such a privileged animal as the Saluki) it would never do for Salukis to be jumping up and licking their owners, or their visitors. Salukis know their place and keep to it while remaining alert to their masters' needs.

Although the Bedouin way of life is fast disappearing, it is to the credit of people like Hamad Al Ghanem, the source of this story, that purebred hunting Salukis continue to be bred as part of the national heritage, to be passed on to the next generation in the same way as the traditions of falconry and horsemanship continue to be preserved. Changing circumstances may mean that, unlike the Hamad of the story, the Hamad of today lives in a house and his Saluki must adapt accordingly, but the remarkable partnership between hunters and their hounds still flourishes in many parts of the Arab world, and long may it remain so.

Sir Terence Clark
Chairman, the Saluki Coursing Club

The boy closed his fist around the pebble. He liked the feel of its cold round smoothness. This was a special pebble. If he had counted correctly it was the sixtieth pebble. He closed his eyes and wished hard before dropping it into the clay bowl, where it nestled amongst the other fifty-nine.

"Perhaps I'd better count them again," he thought, "just to make sure." He took off his *ghutra*, the red and white checked cloth he wore around his head, and spread it out on the sand. He tipped up the bowl and the pebbles rolled out onto the *ghutra*. Carefully he counted them into piles of ten. When he had finished he had made six piles of ten. Yes! Sixty pebbles! He had dropped one into the bowl every morning for sixty days! Grandfather Shaheen had said that they could arrive any time after sixty days had passed.

One by one the boy dropped the pebbles back into the bowl, counting again. The bowl looked satisfyingly full. He shook it gently, enjoying the clunking sound of hard pebbles against the clay. "Soon, soon," he thought, "any day now…"

His dreams were interrupted. "Counting again?" Grandfather Shaheen asked, " it won't make the days pass any faster you know." He chuckled, and cuffed the top of the boy's head.

Jumping up, the boy grabbed his grandfather's hand. "Sixty," he said, "sixty whole days!" "Do you think I don't know," Grandfather replied, "with you counting all the time?!" and he laughed again. "But nature will take its course, Hamad; they'll come when they're ready and not before." "But it must be soon Grandfather," said Hamad, and his heart was beating fast with excitement. "*In sha'allah*," Grandfather said, "God willing."

Those sixty days had seemed to Hamad the longest days of his life. He had watched each changing face of the moon at least twice over, not to mention sixty sunrises and sixty sunsets! He had counted up to sixty in so many different ways: sixty dates on the plate to welcome guests, sixty palm leaf fronds which his mother plaited into a basket, sixty twists of the rope which tethered the goats, sixty lengths of wool for his grandmother to weave into the carpet . . .

"You're driving me crazy!" his mother, Mouzah, had said on more than one occasion! He was driving everyone crazy! Only last night he had woken the entire family! Hearing a rustling noise, he had leapt up from his sleeping mat shouting, "Wake up! Wake up! It's time! They are coming!" But it had only been a mouse stealing rice from the sack! It had taken his mother a long time to calm his small sister, and settle her back to sleep.

But his waiting was not over yet. Two more whole days passed before he was finally rewarded and they arrived.

It happened during the night, as these things so often do. Hamad opened his eyes, and for a few moments he lay in the semi-darkness, wondering what it was that had woken him this time. Could it be another mouse? Or a grasshopper perhaps? He listened to the rhythmic breathing of his parents who were lying close by.

Then he heard a small whimper, and instantly he was wide awake! This was the sound he had been longing to hear! Throwing the rug aside, he got up quietly and tiptoed over to where his Grandfather Shaheen lay sleeping. He patted the old man's hand gently. "Grandfather, Grandfather wake up," he whispered, " I think it's time!" Grandfather rubbed the sleep from his eyes. "Are you sure, Hamad?" he asked. Then he heard the sound as well.

Light from the full moon spilled into the tent through the tear in the goat hair wool, and Hamad could make out the family's two Salukis quite clearly. Dhabian, the male, stood watchful and alert, keeping guard over Reasha, who was panting slightly. Dhabian nuzzled her reassuringly. Boy and grandfather crept over to the Salukis, and knelt down beside them.

It was not long before the first puppy made its appearance. Reasha knew instinctively what to do: she helped it from its slippery bag, and licked it clean. Then she nudged it closer, encouraging it to suckle. Hamad watched. "Will this one become my Saluki?" he wondered. He imagined himself hunting in the desert, his Saluki tearing after a hare, whilst Nahar the falcon soared overhead waiting to dive down for the kill. But his dreams were interrupted! Already a second puppy was arriving. A third followed soon after, and by first light of day the litter was complete. Seven puppies nestled in the shallow sandpit which Grandfather Shaheen had dug for the purpose. He had lined it with old clothes, and now Reasha lay resting contentedly.

"Are you sure that's all, Grandfather?" Hamad asked. "I thought you said she could have as many as eleven." Grandfather ran his experienced hands over Reasha's stomach again. "Seven is more than enough when food is not plentiful," he said, "let us hope they all survive, God willing."

Hamad's father, Ahmed, came into the tent carrying a bowl. "Camel milk," he announced, "to help Reasha regain her strength." He set down the bowl and admired the new arrivals. All but one was fast asleep, exhausted after the big adventure of being born!

It was true that food had been in short supply of late, but Hamad's mother had somehow seen to it that the family never went hungry, and there was always a good smell coming from her cooking pot. That night she prepared a chicken to celebrate the birth of the puppies.

Afterwards they gathered around the fire, and Grandfather Shaheen sang of days gone by. His voice was rich and strong, and he was a wonderful storyteller. Hamad loved to hear him, and his head was filled with pictures as he listened. When Grandfather came to the words of Abu Nawas, the poet, about the Saluki, Hamad joined in:

"Like an arrow it was sent,
Tearing away from his own skin,
Lightning in a cloud."

"*Mabrouk*! You remember well, Hamad!" Grandfather said.

"Do you think that my Saluki will be like that Grandfather? Like an arrow?" Hamad asked. "Well we can hope so, for he is pure bred," Grandfather replied, "but it will be up to you to train him well."

"And that will take patience Hamad," Grandmother Fatima put in, and she chuckled. Hamad was glad that it was dark as he felt his cheeks redden. Patience was not something he had shown much of over the past sixty-two days! And already he was in a hurry for the puppies to grow so that Dhabian and Reasha would make their choices, for both hounds would choose a favourite. It had been decided that Hamad would be given Reasha's choice, for a mother would usually favour the strongest and healthiest of the litter. His very own Saluki! It would become his trusted companion, his loyal friend, and they would work together.

Once again Hamad's head was full of pictures! This time he was returning home with a gazelle, and all the family was coming out to meet him, rejoicing in the catch. His father would be proud of a son who brought such food home to his family. His sister would be impressed, his brothers too! All the family would be invited to celebrate and enjoy the feast!

Grandfather's voice took on a gentler note as he began to sing of Sarab, his most beloved hound. Long departed, but never forgotten, Sarab was fabled throughout the land. Tales of his exploits were sung all over the desert sands. Named after the mirage, his speed and stamina had become legendary. Now Grandfather was singing of the time Sarab had saved a baby from wolves. Hamad knew the story well, but never tired of hearing it. The baby was his own father!

Leaving the baby in the shade of a bush for a moment, Grandmother Fatima had gone inside the tent to fetch something. When she came out the baby had gone! Vanished into thin air! Unable to believe her eyes, she searched frantically. She had not heard the baby cry out. Where could he have gone? How could he have gone? He was too young to crawl. Fear clutched her heart, and she gave a wild howl. Her shrieks and wails carried over the sands, and soon Grandfather came running with other Bedouin at his heels. They tried to calm her, to find out what had happened, but she could only sob, "A *djinn*! A *djinn*! A *djinn* has taken our son!"

16

The men looked at the spot beneath the bush where the baby had lain. Perhaps a branch had been broken and displeased the *djinn* which lived there. And then they saw the tracks! Wolf tracks! And their hearts too were full of fear. But as they followed the wolf tracks, another set of prints became apparent. Hope edged its way into Grandfather's heart, for those were Sarab's paw prints. He recognized them instantly.

The men hurried forward. "Sarab," Grandfather called, and he was rewarded with an answering bark. Over the rise of the dune he sped, and there below was Sarab, keeping guard over a bundle. Miraculously, the baby was unhurt, but Sarab was bleeding from a gash on his shoulder.

Grandfather stopped singing. Emotion silenced his voice. So Grandmother took up the tale, describing the feasting and rejoicing that took place that night. They had killed three goats to feed all the visitors. The story had travelled so fast, that many came to see the famous hound, bringing with them herbs and oils, remedies for his wound.

"Will my hound do something brave and wonderful?" Hamad wondered. There was every chance it would since it was descended from Sarab's bloodline.

That night Hamad's dreams were full of heroic deeds and rescues! But between times he woke up, and lay in the darkness, listening to the snuffles and squeaks and whimpers of the new family! Five times he got up and crept over to the sand box where they lay. He was careful not to bump into anything, feeling his way cautiously so that no one else should waken, but on the fifth occasion he was stopped in his tracks by his father's voice: "Do you think that Dhabian and Reasha cannot manage without you Hamad?" "I'm just making sure that they are all right, Father," Hamad replied. "Five times?" his father asked. Hamad thought for a moment. "It would be terrible if raiders were to come and steal them," he suggested. "It certainly would," his father replied, "but I imagine that Dhabian might bark if a thief were to approach." That was true! "*Djinns* like nothing better than small boys who rise up from their sleeping mats in the night time," his father said. Another voice – his mother's – added, "They always wait for the sixth time." That did it! Hamad did not stir from his mat again that night!

Hamad's days were full! When he was not herding goats, or reciting the Qu'ran under his Grandfather Saqer's guidance, he could be found watching the puppies! To begin with they did little but eat and sleep. Safe in the confines of the box they blindly pushed and shoved one another, jostling for their mother's milk. But two of the puppies were weaker than the others and did not thrive. One morning only five remained. Grandfather buried the two small bodies in the sand beneath a large bush. Hamad accepted this loss philosophically, despite feelings of sadness. Life in the desert has always been harsh.

As the puppies grew, and they opened their eyes, they became more curious, and would climb onto their mother's back to peer over the sides of the sand box. Always they would rush to greet Hamad, wagging their tails eagerly, and yelping with delight. One favoured him more than the rest, and was content to stay at his side as he sat with them. Would this be the chosen one? Hamad rather hoped so, but it would have to be Reasha's choice. So Hamad watched and waited.

There were three males and two females. Each day their features grew more recognizably those of the Saluki hound: the elegant narrow head, the muscular frame and the long legs. One was pure black, another reddish brown, two were the colour of the desert sand, and the fifth was black with brown chest and brown eyebrows. The Bedouin called such a one Four Eyes, because in the black of night all that you would see were the two eyes and the two pale eyebrows! Hamad loved her unusual markings. Although he did not say so, this one was his favourite.

The moon passed through all its changing phases twice more. And then one morning Reasha had made her choice. To Hamad's delight she had singled out the very hound he had set his heart upon. She had chosen Sougha, for that's what he would call his Saluki – Sougha, the Gifted One.

"I see we are of one mind Hamad." Hamad looked up at the sound of Grandfather Shaheen's voice. "Grandfather, this is Sougha," he said proudly. Grandfather stroked the hound's black silky coat. "Sougha," he said, "You were my choice as well as Reasha's, and I know you were Hamad's. We have high hopes for you," and Sougha wagged her tail with pleasure.

From the first there was an understanding between Saluki and boy. Although playful, Sougha was also watchful and obedient, and showed all the signs of becoming a loyal companion. For his part, Hamad was keen to be worthy of the hound's devotion.

Hamad spent long hours patiently training Sougha and the hound was quick to learn. She loved to chase after Hamad's red and white *ghutra* which he pulled in his wake as he ran through the sand. She learnt to sit, and to wait for Hamad's call, "Come, Sougha, come!" before she darted forward to seize the cloth. Then he would reward her with a date.

She loved the sweet, sticky treats, and watched expectantly as Hamad put his hand into his pocket. Sometimes he threw the date up into the air for her to catch. Occasionally he would tease her, and she would leap up high as his hand opened, only to discover that the date was still in his pocket!

Sougha loved to play with her brothers and sister too. They rolled and tumbled together in mock fight. If there was misbehaviour Dhabian or Reasha brought them to order with a sharp bark!

Dhabian had picked out the reddish brown puppy, and Hamad's father named him Jarian. When it came to games, Jarian loved to challenge his sister Sougha. If Hamad threw a stick for Sougha, Jarian would race after it as well. If Sougha reached the stick first, Jarian would pounce on it and try to seize it from her. Several *ghutras* were ripped apart over a tug of war!

SALUKI ~ HOUND OF THE BEDOUIN

When Sougha was introduced to Nahar, the falcon, as he sat on his perch outside the tent, she soon discovered that he was no playmate! His sharp talons, his fierce beak, his unblinking stare, and the smell of blood proclaimed him a hunter. Sougha kept a respectful distance! But she learnt to hunt with Nahar as her partner.

Soon it was time for Sougha's brothers and sister to go their separate ways. It was the Bedouin custom to make gifts of Saluki hounds, and Jarian and the other three puppies had been promised to the families of Ahmed's brothers. Hamad hoped that they would care for the beautiful animals as much as he cared for Sougha.

At first Sougha missed them, but she was busy, and besides she had Hamad! They were rarely apart! When he milked the goats Sougha came too, and if any should stray she would try to round them up. Like all Salukis, she was welcome to sit with the family when they ate, patiently waiting her turn. She quickly came to accept that if her master went hungry when food was in short supply, then she would go hungry as well. But when food was plentiful she would receive her share. Their food was her food.

Sometimes Grandfather trapped a live hare, and released it for Sougha to chase. The first time she caught one, she grabbed it from behind. Thinking to play with it, she opened her jaws. The hare ran away, and she was too tired to chase it again! But she did not make the same mistake twice! The next time she held the hare down and waited for Hamad to retrieve it.

Grandfather and Hamad took the Saluki and the falcon into a steep sided rocky *wadi*, and there she learnt that her job was to flush the hare out into the open, to back off at her master's command, and to leave the kill to Nahar.

Every morning, after the *Fajr* prayers at first light of dawn, Grandfather and Hamad would walk into the sands with the Salukis. Hamad loved to watch Sougha's elegant, high-stepping gait as she trotted by his side. Nahar the falcon, hooded, sat on Grandfather's arm. Under Grandfather's watchful eye, Hamad taught Sougha to walk respectfully at his side, and to follow his commands. Sougha loved to run, and Hamad thrilled to watch her sleek, muscular body catapult into action, her four feet all off the ground at the same time! Soon Sougha would be earning her keep and fulfilling the rule of the Qu'ran, which says that a Muslim should only keep a working animal.

Those mornings were all part of Hamad's education too. At that time of the day, before the scorching heat, and before the wind had covered them with sand, tracks ran hither and thither over the surface of the desert – so many creatures had been out and about and busy during the night: here a scorpion's trail, there the deeper, winding pathway made by a snake. There were paw prints of foxes and of desert hares, and jerboas with long tails. Hamad's grandfather taught him not only to recognize the tracks, but to read the deeper meanings.

29

"So Hamad, what do you make of these?" he asked one morning, pointing to a hare's prints with his camel stick. Hamad knelt down to examine them more closely. The tracks were close together and followed a confused zigzag pathway. "I think the hare must have been sleepy," Hamad offered, "the tracks are further apart when the hare is lively." "Correct," said Grandfather, "and why do you think the prints are not in a straight line?" "Perhaps there was something wrong. It looks as if it couldn't decide whether to carry on or to find somewhere to rest," Hamad ventured. "And so?" Grandfather queried. "So ...," Hamad thought for a moment, "so it's most probably somewhere close by!"

They followed the hare's meandering tracks until they disappeared at a small bush. Sure enough, when they looked beneath the bush there was the hare, sound asleep, its ears folded back against its body. It was startled when Grandfather snatched it up, but he held it firmly in his grasp and it was unable to wriggle free. He examined the hare. "What can you feel, Hamad?" he asked, placing the boy's fingers over the hare's stomach. Hamad touched the hare gently, and he could feel a slight swelling. He also noticed that the teats were enlarged. He smiled, "A female," he said, "and she's carrying babies!" "*Mabrouk*!" Grandfather cried, "you are learning well, Hamad, and you are becoming a useful member of our tribe."

30

Hamad's heart swelled with pride. He thought of his Great Grandfather Ghanem, who was remembered for his ability to read the signs in the sands. A camel's footprint would tell him everything he needed to know from its age, whether it was male or female, if it was hobbled or not, where it had come from and where it was going to, and even how long ago it was since it had passed that way! Many dangerous situations had been successfully avoided thanks to Great Grandfather Ghanem's skills. Perhaps Hamad had inherited those abilities, and would one day become a fearless leader, and his tribe would sing of his amazing adventures!

Hamad pictured himself saving his people from the fangs of snakes, from hostile tribes, from wolves and *djinns* and the terrible sinking sands . . . He tripped over a small bush, and found himself flat on his face! Grandfather pulled him to his feet. "Just look at the great tracker!" he said, and they both laughed.

The bush Hamad had fallen on was a *markh* bush. It was covered with tiny yellow flowers which were good to eat. They gathered some and sat down to enjoy them. It was then that Hamad noticed a small hole beneath the bush. If a *djinn* lived there, he thought, he would be in trouble! The *djinn* would be angry at his clumsiness, and would no doubt take his revenge. Hamad looked at the scattered twigs and leaves, which had broken off when he fell, and shuddered. Grandfather tapped

Hamad's leg with his stick, and putting his finger to his lips, he nodded his head towards the hole. Slowly Hamad turned back to the hole, dreading what he was going to see. But there at the entrance was a little face. Two beady black eyes looked back into Hamad's, a small nose twitched, whiskers quivered.

Sougha was instantly alert and at the ready, waiting for the command to catch it, but Hamad was so grateful to the little creature for being what it was – a jerboa and not a *djinn* – that he had not the heart to kill it. Sougha was disappointed: she had been denied the hare as well, for Allah would surely frown upon anyone foolish enough to kill a pregnant female. The babies would grow to become food for the future. However, on the way home Sougha had her opportunity.

Grandfather always liked to rest at the top of his favourite dune, and look out over the vast sandy emptiness that stretched away in dips and curves as far as the eye could see. He set the falcon down, and lit his *madwakh*, his small wooden pipe, and boy and Grandfather sat together enjoying the desert's unique peace and stillness. The Salukis sat beside them. Sougha's slender, elegant head rested on her forepaws. Hamad stroked her feathered ears and ran his hand the length of her sleek, lean body. She was all muscle, but her coat was soft and silky and she was warm to touch. She was everything a Saluki should be! Grandfather had measured her. "Three fingers width across the top of her head between her ears, and my four fingers fit precisely within the spread of her hips," he had declared with satisfaction, "her chest is wide and deep, we could not ask for better Hamad." But Sougha had yet to prove herself.

Suddenly Hamad felt the Saluki's body tense beneath his hand. Sougha sat up and stared into the distance. Dhabian and Reasha were instantly alert as well. Hamad followed their gaze. Then he looked at his grandfather. Their eyes met, and a look of understanding passed between them. Taking up the falcon, Grandfather followed Hamad, and eagerly they scrambled down the dune.

Only the Salukis knew the prey that awaited them. Not for nothing are they known as sight-hounds. Sougha was ready to go, but it was too early yet, and she obediently ran alongside Hamad, true to her training.

As they sped across the sand, a small bush came into view in the distance. Closer still, and Hamad could just make out a shape beneath it. It was another hare, a big male. No reason this time to deny Sougha! Grandfather unhooded the falcon. Nahar blinked in the bright sunlight. His head bobbed up and down, his eyes darted this way and that, he spread his wings and his shrill screech cut the air. Released in the name of Allah, the falcon soared high into the air. "Go Dhabian! Go Reasha!" Grandfather cried, and Hamad joined in, "Go Sougha!"

Now they really
saw what Sougha was
made of! The hare was
flushed from its lair. Like coiled
springs, Sougha's long legs leapt
into action, her form becoming a blur
as her power-packed body wove this way
and that at high speed in the wake of the
hare. Grandfather and Hamad watched with
mounting excitement.

The hare was strong and fast, and this was a real test of Sougha's stamina. She showed no sign of tiring as she kept up with the older, more experienced hounds. At one moment she even seemed to be edging ahead, but when Hamad called her back she obeyed his command, and the kill was left to the falcon. Nahar dived. It was over!

Grandfather retrieved the falcon, giving it a small piece of the meat, whilst withdrawing the rest of the hare. Then he turned to the Salukis, "Well done, Dhabian! Good girl, Reasha!" and to Sougha he said, "My, my, Sougha, I think you are going to make a fine hunter. *Mabrouk*, Hamad, you are training her well!" Hamad grinned, as he patted the hound's head, and Sougha wagged her tail with pleasure.

And so it was decided, a few months later, that Sougha was ready for the great hunt!

The hunt would involve many of the men and women of the tribe, and they would be away for several days and nights. The preparations began! Hamad's mother made small round balls of goat's cheese, which she dried in the sun. His grandmothers made yogurt and flat bread. Hamad went back and forth to the well many times to fill the goatskins with water. Even his small sister helped by filling up bags with dates and dried meat.

SALUKI ~ HOUND OF THE BEDOUIN

Hamad's older married brothers, his many cousins and uncles travelled from other parts of the sands to join the hunting party. They came on their camels, their hooded falcons on their arms, their Salukis running alongside. Amidst joyful cries of greeting they came, bearing gifts of cloth and sandalwood and *oudh*.

Sougha barked her welcome and wagged her tail. A great feast awaited the guests, and the delicious aroma of roasting meat filled the air.

That evening the men rubbed *henna* into their hair and onto their hands and feet to protect themselves from the burning heat of the sun and the sand in the days to come. The legs of the Salukis were covered too. The ritual was as old and as symbolic as the painting of a bride's hands and feet before her marriage.

Later, gathered around the fire, burners were passed from hand to hand, and the perfumed smoke of the *oudh* drifted amongst them and scented their garments. Sougha, as usual, was beside her master. Hamad looked into her deep, amber eyes and dreamed of the days to come. He was eager for all to see Sougha's skill and stamina in the chase, and he knew that the Saluki sensed his excitement.

One of Hamad's cousins was a boy of about his age called Fahad. Slightly taller than Hamad, he had a superior air about him, and he loved nothing better than to brag of his achievements. He could climb a palm tree "Right to the top," he could dig the deepest well, he could remove the sting of a scorpion with his teeth and he could wrestle a snake! If his stories were to be believed there was no end to the things he could do! Hamad could hear him now: "You should see my hound run," he was saying to no one in particular, "there is nothing faster on four legs than Jarian!" Hamad recognized the red-brown hound sitting by Fahad. And when he looked closer there was the tattoo, the mark of the tribe on the hound's back leg. Of course! it was Sougha's brother! Sougha knew him too, and wagged her tail. They nuzzled each other delightedly.

"Jarian, the Runner, will bring down a gazelle, just you wait and see!" Fahad went on. Hamad was about to say, "Wait till you see Sougha run," but thought better of it. "I think Dhabian made the right choice," Fahad went on, "I was given the prize!" Hamad opened his mouth. He caught Grandfather Shaheen's eye, and shut it again!

The following morning the camels drank long and hard to sustain them for the days ahead. Pulling them down to kneel on the sand, they were loaded up with bags of food and water, with coffee pots and cooking pots. Bright woven rugs were thrown across their backs, and the men and boys were ready to mount.

Hamad went to his tent to say goodbye to his mother and to Heya, his small sister. Hugging him to her, his mother hung a turquoise ring on a length of string around his neck, "To ward off the evil eye," she told him. There was one for Sougha too. Hamad waved to his mother as his camel carried him away from the oasis. He could feel Fahad watching him, but he did not care.

The hunting party travelled deep into the sands, with the sun for their guide. On journeys such as these they kept their eyes open for trees or bushes or changes of colour in the sands which might indicate the presence of water, for one day the water in their oases would run dry and they would have to move on.

During the heat of the day the creatures of the desert hid themselves away, but before the setting of the sun the men came across the tracks of a houbara bustard. Grandfather Shaheen pointed out some bushes which are good for camels, so the party dismounted to allow them to feed, whilst they gathered wood for the fire. Sougha was instantly drawn to one particular bush. With her keen sight she had already noticed a slight movement in the bush. Sure enough the bird was sitting beneath it!

Grandfather and some of the other men unhooded their falcons, and the chase was on!

45

Over the next few days Sougha proved her worth for all to see. She was praised for her obedience, for her stamina and for her speed, and Hamad felt proud. But bringing down a gazelle made her famous!

The herd was far off in the distance, the delicate beige-white colour of the creatures barely visible against the sand. A faint wisp of dust hovered in the air from the animals' hooves. That's what Dhabian must have seen. Instantly alert, his excitement spread to the other hounds like fire!

Sougha looked at Hamad, eagerly awaiting his command to run. But they were still too far away. Closer they ran and closer, until at last Grandfather gave the shout "Go Dhabian, go!" Within a moment of one another Hamad and Fahad released their hounds. "Show them, Jarian," Hamad heard Fahad say, "show them which of you is the prize!" Men, women and boys tore after the hounds! The gazelle were running now, leaping and scattering in different directions. Skilfully, Dhabian separated one of them from the rest of the herd, whilst Jarian ran after another gazelle. But Hamad's eyes were fixed on Sougha. She seemed about to choose a gazelle of her own, but thought better of it. Instead she followed the example of her father, trusting his experience in the hunt. Suddenly she was ahead! Hamad marvelled at her speed and her agility. Her lean body and long slender limbs were built for moments like this.

As the gazelle twisted and turned, so did Sougha. Hamad had never seen her run so fast! With a final lunge, she caught the black tip of the gazelle's tail. That was enough! It stumbled and fell. Dhabian came to the younger hound's assistance, and leapt forward to hold the gazelle down, and Jarian joined them.

The three Salukis sat panting, as they waited patiently for their masters.

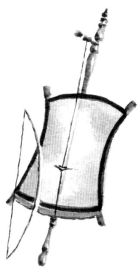

That night was the first of many in which Sougha was celebrated in song. Gathered around the fire, encircled by the camels, the men's words floated into the starlit sky to the accompaniment of the *rababa* and the drum. But Fahad scowled. He had said that his hound was the best, and he was determined to prove it.

One morning Hamad woke to find that Fahad was missing. It was Sougha who noticed first, for Jarian had also gone. Fahad's father was worried. Grandfather Shaheen looked worried too. He could see the boy's footprints and those of the hound disappearing into the desert. A third set of tracks caught his eye. Hamad saw them too. So Fahad was hunting his own gazelle! "That way lie the sinking sands," Grandfather said quietly, but Hamad heard him. "Sougha will find them," Hamad said, and the others agreed. "Sister will find brother," they said, and they knelt on the sand and prayed to Allah that this should be so.

Hamad, his grandfather and Fahad's father set out. Sougha led the way. "We are on camels and they are on foot, we should soon catch up with them," Fahad's father said hopefully. But he was wrong!

Before they had gone far, a terrible wind blew up. It spun across the desert, whipping up the sand into a choking fog. The two men and the boy wrapped their *ghutras* around their faces.

They sat in the protective circle of the camels, and dug themselves into the sand with the hound, and waited for the *shamal* to pass. But when it died away at last, there was not a track to be seen! Neither footprint of boy nor hound remained. And the sun was hidden by the clouds. They did not know which way to go.

Grandfather led them to higher ground, and from there they could just make out their camp far off in the distance. So they walked in the opposite direction, away from the camp, hoping it was the right way, the way to Fahad and Jarian.

Towards evening they climbed another high dune. Grandfather recognized the place. "What is it?" asked Fahad's father. "We are nearing the sinking sands," Grandfather replied. Hamad felt afraid. Gone were his visions of heroic deeds! The sinking sands! He had heard terrible stories of the sinking sands. *Djinns* waited there to suck you slowly into the deep. Once they had hold of you they did not let go. They pulled you down little by little, gradually drowning you in sand. Travellers had lost their lives in the sinking sands, hounds and camels too. One step too far and you disappeared for ever. Hamad shivered!

Sougha's ears were twitching. She stood upright on the dune, peering hard into the distance. Her tail began to wag. Had she seen a hare? Another houbara perhaps? A gazelle? Didn't she understand that they weren't looking for game now, they were looking for Fahad and Jarian? But she was off! She turned back once to make sure the men were following her.

Hamad ran hard. He managed to keep Sougha in view, and suddenly he was rewarded by the sight of a second Saluki. It was not a hare, a houbara or a gazelle which Sougha had seen. It was Jarian! Sougha paused for a moment. She lifted her left front paw and her tail went up. Hamad knew that she was thinking. Then she was off again. "Don't worry Hamad, she's following Jarian's tracks," Grandfather called. "But the sands, Grandfather, what about the sinking sands?" and Hamad felt an icy tingle of fear. In the distance he could see the sands gradually changing colour. He swallowed his fear and tore after Sougha. "If she is brave, then I must be brave too," he thought to himself.

Sougha stopped suddenly. She stood over something and barked. Panting for breath, Hamad caught up with her. There, nearly buried in the sand, just the red and white tip showing through, was Fahad's *ghutra*, the checked cloth he wore wrapped around his head. Hamad froze! He watched Sougha digging, sending clouds of sand into the air. Grandfather and Fahad's father reached the spot. Fahad's father got down on his knees and frantically dug the sand too, searching for his son. But the cloth was all that remained.

Jarian, having regained his breath, was hurrying back towards them. He wagged his tail and barked. Sougha stopped digging. She listened hard. And then they all heard it, a faint cry. "Fahad," his father called, "Fahad!" From far away came the answering call, "Father!"

This time Jarian led the way. On the edge of the sinking sands they found him. Fahad lay in a hollow dug by his Saluki, unable to move, for he had fallen and twisted his ankle.

Fahad's father was about to reach out to his son, but Sougha's commanding bark held him back. Coiled up in front of his cousin, Hamad could see a huge snake. It was a deadly viper! The hounds' hackles rose and their fur stood on end. But they were smarter than the snake! Together they worked to outwit it. As Jarian distracted the viper, Sougha pounced. Seizing it in her jaws, she hurled it high into the air. The snake hung there for a moment, its twisted silhouette black against the sky, before it fell into the sinking sands and disappeared for ever.

That all happened many years ago. But the stories remain. Hamad's children like to hear them. "Tell us about Sougha and the snake," they say, "and about Uncle Fahad." Hamad smiles to himself. He and Fahad are good friends – Sougha and Jarian saw to that!

Hamad continues to sit on the high dune looking out towards the sinking sands. He remembers Sougha. He strokes the camel stick in his hands. It belonged to his grandfather, and he remembers the time when his grandfather gave it to him. But that's another story …

Now he must go home. Sixty days have passed, sixty sunrises, sixty sunsets, twice he has watched each changing face of the moon, and the waiting is almost over.

GLOSSARY

djinn	A spirit. The Qu'ran says the *djinn* were created of 'smokeless fire'. Some are good and others are evil. The English word 'genie' is derived from the Arabic word
fajr	The dawn prayers
ghutra	A red and white checked cloth, worn on the head
henna	A shrub whose leaves are crushed to a paste which is used for dyeing hair, decorating hands and feet on special occasions, and for protection from the sun
houbara	A large bird of the bustard family, and the main game bird hunted by the Bedouin with the Saluki and the falcon
jerboa	A desert rodent which has very long hind legs for jumping
In sha'allah	God willing
Qu'ran	The holy book of Islam
Muslim	A follower of Islam
markh bush	A desert bush whose flowers are edible
madwakh	A small wooden pipe
mabrouk	Congratulations
mirage	An optical illusion in the desert, which makes people imagine they see water
oasis	A fertile place in the desert where water is found
oudh	An expensive wood which is burnt to release its perfume, used at weddings and other special occasions
rababa	A simple stringed instrument
sandalwood	A fragrant East Indian wood
shamal	A northerly wind, bearing sand
wadi	A valley or river bed, usually dry, except after heavy rainfall

Other children's titles from
STACEY INTERNATIONAL

A is for Arabia
Julia Johnson
Illustrated by Emily Styles

£8.50
ISBN: 1 900988 550

One Humpy Grumpy Camel
Julia Johnson
Illustrated by Emily Styles

£8.50
ISBN: 1 900988 755

The Pearl Diver
Julia Johnson
Illustrated by Patricia Al Fakhri

£9.99
ISBN: 1 900988 585

The Cheetah's Tale
Julia Johnson
Illustrated by Susan Keeble

£12.50
ISBN: 1 900988 879

A Gift of the Sands
Julia Johnson
Illustrated by Emily Styles

£9.95
ISBN: 1 900988 917

The Children's Encyclopaedia of Arabia
Mary Beardwood

£19.95
ISBN: 1 900988 33X